A FROG and DOG book
Un libro de RANA y PERRO

Frog
Meets
Dog

Rana
conoce
Perro

Janee Trasler

ACORN™
SCHOLASTIC INC.

For Miles, with love from Andy Janee.

Para Miles, con cariño de Andy Janee.

Originally published in English as *Frog Meets Dog*

ISBN 978-1-338-71551-4

14 13 12 11 10 9 8 7   23 24 25 26 27

Printed in India   197

First Spanish edition, 2021

Book design by Sunny Lee

Dog
Perro

Dog wants to play.
Perro quiere jugar.

2

Frogs hop. Can Dog hop too?
Las ranas dan saltitos.
¿Puede Perro dar saltitos también?

Hop
Saltito

Hop
Saltito

Hop
Saltito

5

Frogs leap. Can Dog leap too?

Las ranas saltan.
¿Puede Perro saltar también?

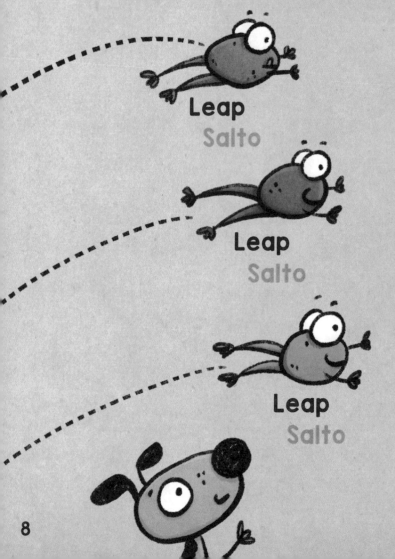

Leap
Salto

Leap
Salto

Leap
Salto

9

DEEP HONDO

Frogs jump. Can Dog jump too?

Las ranas brincan.
¿Puede Perro brincar también?

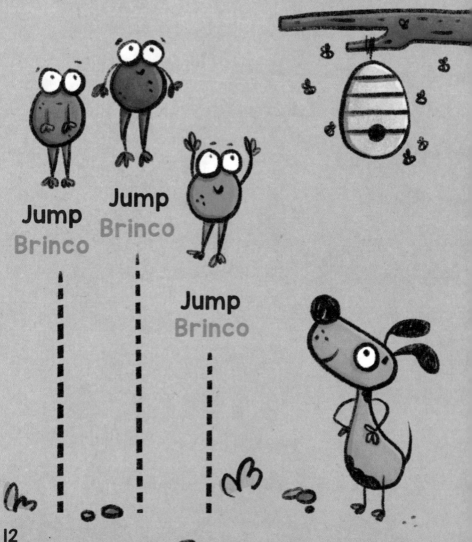

Jump
Brinco

Jump
Brinco

Jump
Brinco

12

13

Dog will play another day.

Perro jugará otro día.

Frogs jump.
Las ranas brincan.

21

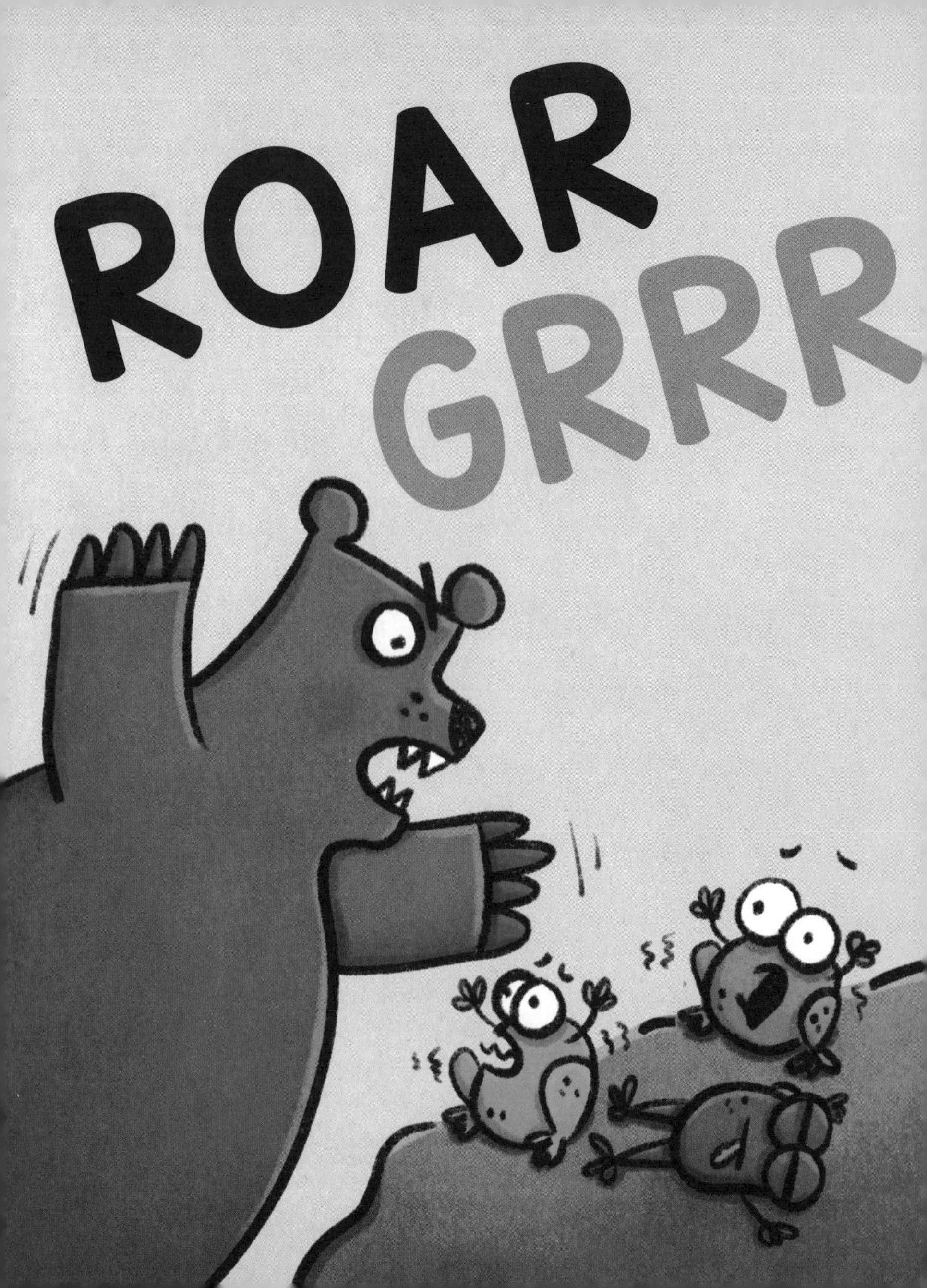
ROAR
GRRR

Dog wants to help.
How can Dog help?

Perro quiere ayudar.
¿Cómo puede Perro ayudar?

Jump
Brinco

Jump
Brinco

Jump
Brinco

27

Frogs want to play.
Las ranas quieren jugar.

Frogs hop. Can Dog hop too?

**Las ranas dan saltitos.
¿Puede Perro dar saltitos también?**

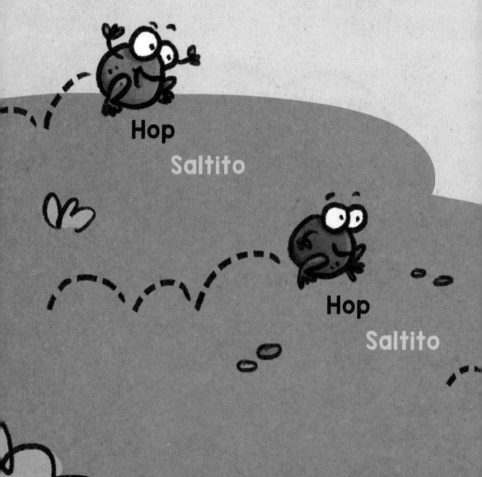

Hop

Saltito

Hop

Saltito

Hop

Saltito

33

POP
PAF

DROP

CAÍDA

Frogs jump. Can Dog jump too?

Las ranas brincan.
¿Puede Perro brincar también?

Jump
Brinco

Jump
Brinco

Jump
Brinco

36

Lump

Chichón

Frogs leap. Can Dog leap too?

Las ranas saltan.
¿Puede Perro saltar también?

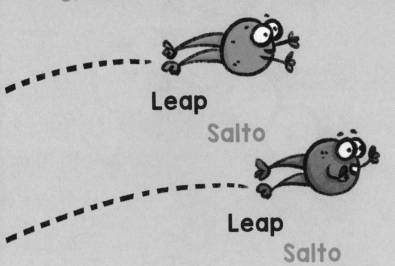

Leap

Salto

Leap

Salto

Leap

Salto

Heap
Pila

Sleep
Dormir

Bzzzzz . . .
Zzzzzz. . .

Frog wants to eat.
Rana quiere comer.

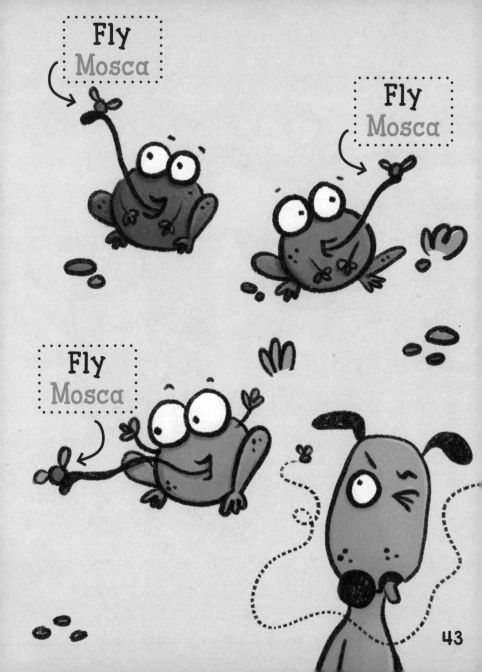

Dog will play another day.
Perro jugará otro día.

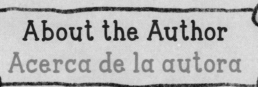

About the Author
Acerca de la autora

Janee Trasler loves to make kids laugh. Whether she is writing books, drawing pictures, singing songs, or performing with her puppets, she is going for the giggle. Janee lives in Texas with her hubby, her doggies, and one very squeaky guinea pig.

A **Janee Trasler** le encanta hacer reír a los niños. Ya sea escribiendo libros, haciendo dibujos, cantando o manejando títeres, ese es siempre su objetivo. Janee vive en Texas con su esposo, sus perritos y un conejillo de Indias muy chillón.

DRAW FROG! / ¡DIBUJA A RANA!

1 Draw a sideways figure 8.
Dibuja un número 8 inclinado.

2 Add a dot in the middle of each circle. Draw a "u" for the mouth.
Añade un punto a cada círculo. Dibuja una "u" para la boca.

3 Connect the eyes with a big circle for the body.
Dibuja un gran círculo para el cuerpo.

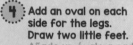

4 Add an oval on each side for the legs. Draw two little feet.
Añade un óvalo a cada lado para las patas. Dibuja las patitas.

5 Draw the arms and hands. Be sure to add some speckles!
Dibuja los brazos y las manos. ¡Asegúrate de añadir manchas!

6 Color in your drawing!
¡Colorea tu dibujo!

WHAT'S YOUR STORY?
¿CUÁL ES TU CUENTO?

Dog plays with the frogs.
Imagine you are playing with them.
What games would you play together?
Write and draw your story!

Perro juega con las ranas.
Imagina que tú eres quien juega con ellas.
¿A qué juegos jugarían?
¡Escribe y dibuja el cuento!